A Boy Called Chipmunk

ISBN 978-1-64349-091-5 (paperback)
ISBN 978-1-64349-092-2 (digital)

Christian Faith Publishing, Inc.
832 Park Avenue
Meadville, PA 16335
www.christianfaithpublishing.com

Printed in the United States of America

A Boy Called Chipmunk

Judy A. Goelitz

Hi! My friends call me Chipmunk.

You might think that's really strange, but let me explain.

Chipmunk is my nickname.

A nickname is a name your friends or family call you that isn't your real name.

It's sort of an extra name.

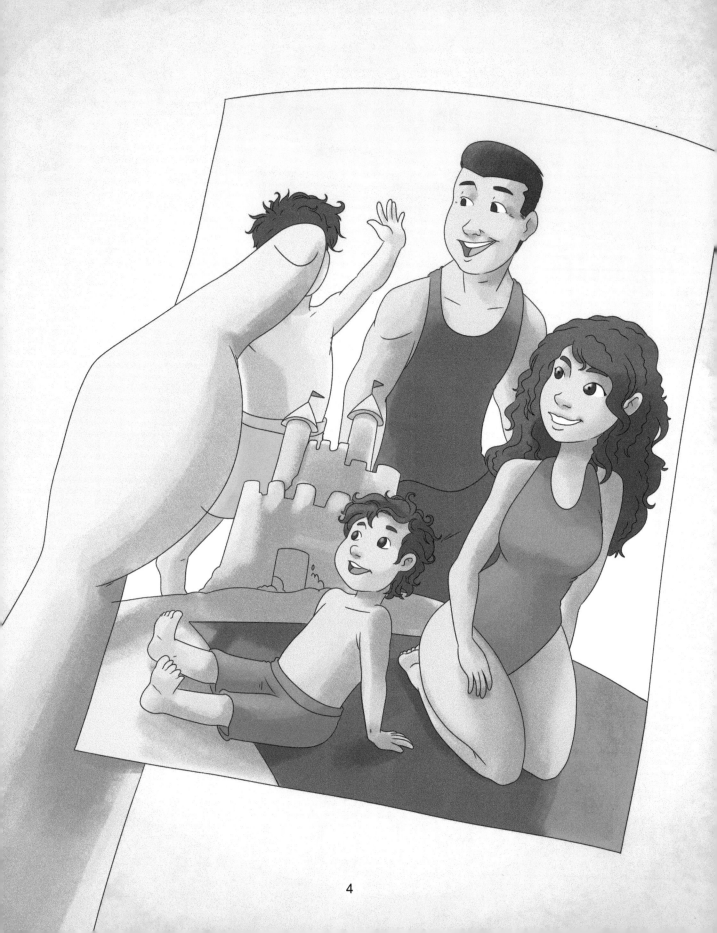

You see, everyone has a name,
and some people have two or more.

A nickname can be a name that shows how
someone feels about you.

My Dad's name is Frank, but my mom just calls him Darling or Honey.

Yuck!

My Dad calls my mom Poopsie.
He says it's a sweetheart name.

I just roll my eyes.

9

Everyone calls my Uncle Philip, Pete.
I don't know why.

Dad says it's just for Pete's sake.

My friend Tyler also answers to Bud.
He's my best buddy. He has a lot of friends.

Sometimes a nickname is based on something about your body. Or a nickname can even be something you are not.

My baby brother Aaron has really red hair. Mom calls him Little Red.

My friend Sam is taller than any other guy in our class. We all call him Shorty.

Sometimes people have a nickname based on what they like to do.

A fierce football player might be called Crusher.

A girl who likes to dress up all the time might be called Princess.

Mom says it is important to not give someone a nickname that makes them feel bad. It's mean to make fun of how people look or act.

Nicknames should be fun!

In baseball, George Ruth was called Babe or the Bambino.

Sometimes a nickname is just
making your name shorter or longer,
like calling my friend Johnathon,
John or Johnny.

A nickname can even be just changing
your real name a little.

My friend Jessica's sister calls her Jessie.

A man named Henry is often called Hank.

I really like my nickname.

My real name is Christopher Munkowski, but my mom and dad just call me Chip.

My friends call me Chipmunk.

Get it?

About the Author

Judy Goelitz is a happily married mother of two teenagers. She has always loved to read and is thrilled to publish her first book. Her own childhood nickname is in this book. Can you guess which one it is?

CPSIA information can be obtained
at www.ICGtesting.com
Printed in the USA
LVHW070109240419
615328LV00038B/1162/P

9 781643 490915